8:59:29

POLLY SCHATTEL

TREPIDATIO
PUBLISHING

ISBN: 978-1-68510-078-0 (sc)
ISBN: 978-1-68510-079-7 (ebook)
Library of Congress Catalog Number: 2022951266

Printed by Trepidatio Publishing in the United States of America.
Cover Design: Don Noble
Editing and Cover/Interior Layout by Scarlett R. Algee
Proofreading by Sean Leonard

Trepidatio Publishing, an imprint of JournalStone Publishing
3205 Sassafras Trail
Carbondale, Illinois 62901

Trepidatio books may be ordered through booksellers or by contacting:
JournalStone | www.journalstone.com

To Jacob. I love you, old man.

8:59:29

one

WHEN HETTA SALTER asked her students, "What's the difference between film and video—the real difference?" none of them could tell her. The faces looking back at her were defeated, vacant, a liminal space of young humanity. This was *Film Studies for Non-Majors*, which meant Hetta got everyone but the serious future filmmakers she wanted. She got the listless athletes and the distracted party girls and the creepy chemistry kids, she got the chatters and the yawners and the snoozers and the mousy good girls who gave it their best but it just wasn't their thing. Once, Hetta had a young woman who actually paid attention, who showed real promise as a screenwriter, but one time the girl leaned too far back in her chair in class and fell and broke her coccyx, and she dropped out.

"The primary difference," Hetta said, pacing back and forth near the whiteboard at the front of the room, "is that film is a chemical medium, pretty much just silver halide crystals dancing on squares of cellulose acetate. Which are typically eight, sixteen, thirty-five or sometimes even sixty-five millimeters in size."

She paused for a moment, looking for signs of life in their eyes. She hadn't lost all of them quite yet, but she was well on her way.

"Video, on the other hand, is an electronic medium that was for a long time not even a whole image, but instead a series of intermeshed fields, an A field and a B field, which together made an image." To demonstrate, she laced her fingers together and made a screen of them.

"Film, of course, is traditionally shown at 24 frames per second, while video's electronic fields are refreshed at 23.98, 29.97, or even 59.94 times a second."

The kids stared at her, unmoved and unmoving, aside from the girl in the front row who was making herself up as carefully as a Las Vegas showgirl. Thank God for Tanner, her only truly engaged student. But Tanner wasn't here today, which was odd. Tanner was here every day. His empty seat in the back corner glared at her. She felt his absence the way a tongue feels a missing tooth.

Hetta went to the whiteboard. "Now listen. Frame rate is the duration of individual images, right? Back in the early days of video, when it was black and white only, it ran at an exact thirty frames per second." She drew a big *30* in her sloppy handwriting. "But when *color* was introduced in 1954, the limitations of the circuits in those old television sets required the frame rate to be slowed slightly, to 29.97 images per second." She scratched out the *30* and wrote *29.97*. "Any questions?"

There were none. She was conscious of their breathing, their shifting, their restlessness.

"So, if you do the math, a frame rate of 29.97 is 99.9 percent as fast as 30 frames per second. This microscopic slowdown of frames naturally causes a disparity between the measurement of real time and video time. As we know, real time keeps on ticking, but because of that slight slowdown, video machines like TVs and editing programs and video projectors, they just skip the first two frames of every minute. To keep it playing at full speed, there's a tiny blip in there—two frames every minute get eaten, dropped, overlooked."

She paused again. The silence of their stares was almost spooky.

"Where do they go? For all practical purposes, they just"—Hetta snapped her fingers—"disappear into the ether."

Just then there was a gentle knock on the classroom door. Without waiting for an answer, it opened, and Hensley poked his head in. "Hi, sorry to bother everyone. You all look so smart!"

Hetta didn't reply. Dr. Hensley was the department chair, and everyone knew the head of the film program wouldn't poke his head into a class unless there was an issue. He pointed a finger gun at Hetta. "Hey, can I buy you lunch later? Say, one o'clock?"

"Um, of course," Hetta said. She felt the students studying her reaction. Finally, they were interested in something. "Is there an issue?"

"Nah, we'll talk in a bit." Hensley gave her the thinnest of smiles. "As you were." The door closed as gently as it had opened.

Hetta thought, *Fuck fuck fuck.*

***

The meeting pressed upon her all morning. It felt heavy, she dreaded it the way you dread getting a letter in the mail from the IRS, nothing good came from a meeting with Hensley. When she knocked on his office door, she was still hoping against hope that maybe the whole thing would get delayed or even cancelled. *Dr. J. Walter Hensley*, his door said. It chafed her modest sensibilities that he called himself that—*Dr.*, that anyone would call themselves *Dr.* It was a like a carpenter introducing themselves as *Master Wheelwright* or a plumber calling themselves *Pipefitter Supreme*. Hensley was born rich, of course he was, his father had been a concert pianist and it had been assumed, he'd told Hetta once during a liquored-up staff party, that he would merely follow in his father's footsteps. Hensley liked to tickle the old ivories a bit himself. But he'd settled on academia instead—more security, he told her, which she thought was a joke. Why would J. Walter Hensley need security? He'd practically been born with a mortarboard on his head.

Hetta, on the other hand, wasn't so lucky. She would have loved to pursue her own doctorate, but by her last year of her undergrad, desperation and futility had taken over as the true taskmasters of her life. Leukemia had chewed up her father's already scrawny body—emaciated as it was from the alcoholism—and her mother had been nearly a decade gone. And by then Hetta was so mucked up in the quicksand of federal student loans she couldn't realistically take it any further. The thwarted ambition, the aborted business of constructing a real career, had grown inward, had oxidized in her brain, it rusted her and caused pieces of her to flake off. She imagined herself leaving trails of angry dust wherever she went.

She heard Hensley's footsteps approach, and then the door opened. "Hetta," he said with his usual priggish half-smile, "come." His office, tastelessly lit by the overhead fluorescents, was as charmless as a DMV waiting room. "Got you a turkey sub," he said, "hope that's all right."

She shrugged. Working lunches were either a lousy meal or a lousy meeting, or both. They went over to the table in the corner, where two lunch bags sat waiting for them. "Water's over there," Hensley said, pointing to the dispenser.

Hetta sat and unwrapped her sandwich and looked at it while Hensley attacked his own. "So," he said with a mouthful, "I'm sorry for barging in on you like that, but I want you to know we're getting complaints from some of your kids."

Hetta felt her neck and her shoulders tense up, but said nothing. She didn't like talking about whether she was doing a good job or not. She worked as hard as she could, and frankly, those kids—most of them as smugly entitled as Hensley himself—were horrible judges of what was good or bad. What did they know of the real world, of bad luck and tenacity and lack? What did they know of sick parents and bedpans and struggle and despair?

"It's not a huge deal," Hensley was saying, "and I won't let it turn into one. But I wanted you to know that some of the kids are not happy. And this is on top of the last few semesters—some seriously disgruntled kids there too, Hetta. You've read your evals. It's bad enough for me to bring it up to you."

"Who's disgruntled?"

"I can't tell you that. And I know you know that." Hensley picked a tomato from his sandwich and dropped into his mouth from above, like feeding a baby bird. "But some of the kids are feeling…um, *browbeaten*. As if you don't respect them or their, you know, their knowledge."

"Their *knowledge*?" Hetta made herself look at him, to face him. She couldn't afford to lose this job. Not that it paid well—adjuncting was poverty wages, it was like this everywhere, and it wasn't unheard of that some adjuncts were literally homeless. Not her, thank god, she had a tiny apartment an hour away on the rough side of the city, but it wasn't always a sure thing. She had no tenure, she was on her own, and adjuncting at UNSC wasn't exactly setting her career on fire.

"They don't know a whole lot, Walt," Hetta said, parsing carefully. "That's why they're here. Especially since most of these kids are just"—she didn't want to say it, but she couldn't not—"…new-money dickwads."

It was true. There had been a recent influx of cash into the northern part of the state as land prices and vacation tourism boomed. With great hiking nearby, and camping and whitewater rivers, what had once been a relatively quiet, rural part of the state was now seeing an explosion of vacationers and breweries and second-home trust-funders. The tiny towns with their narrow winding streets had filled up with rap-blaring SUVs roaring past gated communities full of McMansions. It was all, Hetta thought, unspeakably despicable.

"All right, look. I know you think most of the decent kids went off to State." Hensley wiped his mouth with a paper towel. "But that doesn't mean the ones who are here are simple. They're just young, Hetta. We're changing their lives. Opening them up to new things." She watched him struggling not to give her a sour look, and fail. "And anyway, you're here to *arouse* their curiosity, not judge them or intimidate them about what they don't know."

"I'm trying to make it demanding, Walt. If it's not a challenge, it's not worth doing. The rigor is the point."

"But you gotta lose the attitude. We're here to help them, not to make them miserable." Hensley pushed his sandwich away, as if it was suddenly making him sick. Hetta hadn't yet taken a bite out of her own food. It looked oily and soggy, and anyway, she was thinking she might save it for dinner.

"And another thing," Hensley said. "People are talking about someone in your class, some unregistered kid. A local. Are people auditing your class, Hetta?"

Tanner. Hensley was talking about Tanner. Tanner was a townie, not one of the rich kids who greased their way into a small-town party school. No, Tanner really was low-income, from a homegrown hill family, and decidedly *not* meant for the academy. But Hetta had seen a kind of raw talent in him…which may have only been enthusiasm, yes, but in her heart Hetta considered those two to be pretty close to the same thing. Tanner *wanted* to be a filmmaker. When he was enrolled as a freshman, he'd taken her elective until he couldn't keep up with his tuition, and he dropped out. Hetta felt sorry for him, and sorry for herself that the only interesting student she had was being removed.

"No one's auditing my class," she said defensively.

"Community kid." Hensley consulted a piece of paper. "Daryl…Tanner."

He was right. After that last class, Hetta and Tanner had come to an arrangement—*don't ask, don't tell.* But keep coming, and keep learning. And so he did. It was okay with Hetta. Tanner knew the difference between film and video. "I know who you're talking about," she admitted.

"So what's going on?"

Slowly, reluctantly, she explained to Hensley the situation—that she'd had, for once in her time here, a truly talented kid in her class, a local from the hills outside town, a teen with no prospects and no way out. Kinda like herself. Learning the film trade would be his way out.

Hensley smiled at the nerve of it. "You know that breaks about fifty of our rules and student-slash-faculty protocols, don't you?"

"I—I was trying to help. He's—well, he's low-income. Really low-income." In her lap, her hands felt useless and cold. "He needs some help, and I was in a position to do it. It's not like he disrupts the class or anything."

This wasn't entirely true. Tanner spoke up often and at length. Hetta suspected he sometimes came in stoned, you could hear it in the slur of his voice and the random, almost non-linear free-flow of his ideas. And sometimes his and Hetta's conversations on some obscure filmmaker or bygone technique would dominate the class, and at the end of it she would glance up, seeing the rest of the pasty faces staring at her, their eyes even glassier than normal, like a menagerie of dolls.

"If he's not *enrolled*, Hetta," Hensley said, "he's not a student. Period. These kids—*their parents*—pay a lot of money for them to be here." The annoyance, always close in his voice, was unmistakable. "We got rid of him, Hetta. He's not coming back."

Hetta nodded, feeling spanked. Damn. Class without Tanner would be dull indeed.

Hensley took off his glasses, his eyes red and puffy with frustration. His eyelashes were as blonde as his eyebrows. "Frankly, Hetta, I gotta say, I'm a bit disappointed. When we brought you on we thought we were getting an actual film writer, a real critic, and even a genuine, working filmmaker. But in the three years you've been here, you quit whatever writing job you had, you haven't had a single publication that I know of, nor have you made a film. Not even a short. If you'd managed to carve out a higher profile for yourself, I could see giving you more room to roam. But you haven't, and we aren't. As it is, I'm left defending your hire to my bosses, and between you and me, they're looking at other possible adjuncts to bring on. Adjuncts who don't get complaints of surly behavior and letting local kids attend their classes for free."

Hetta didn't argue. He had a point; things had taken a turn for the worse just about the time she started this job. She chalked most of it up to depression—her longtime partner Robby had told her he didn't want to be in "this manner of relationship" with her anymore, whatever that meant. He'd moved out, and within weeks he'd completely disappeared. Hetta'd been ghosted. But for what? The ensuing emotional rockslide in her life was brutal—a long, subterranean stint of gloom Hetta wasn't sure she'd emerged from just yet.

"I have to wonder, Hetta, whether you misrepresented yourself to us. Or padded your CV. At this point, I'm honestly wondering if any of your accolades are real."

"*Padded my CV?*" she said. A dull thumping had begun in her chest, which she knew by now was rising irritation and adrenaline. But she would only really feel it later, after the meeting had ended. Tonight there would be headaches and stress-cricks, which pissed her off even more. "You don't think I did what I said I did?"

"All I know is I'm getting complaints left and right, and you're letting kids take your class who aren't even enrolled here. What is this?"

She sat back and crossed her arms like a toddler. *Hetta Salter, wielder of words, of ideas so sharp they could cut you, getting complaints from ditzy daddy's girls and pickup-truck momma's boys? Who gives a royal flying fuck?* She wanted to stand up, to storm out, to make a point. But she didn't. She needed this job.

Hensley saw her frustration. Whatever else he was, J. Walter Hensley wasn't dumb. "You can't quit," he warned her. "You signed a contract. You're good through the entire semester. If you walk out now and leave us holding the bag, your teaching career is over."

Teaching career? a voice in her head cackled, *what teaching career?* But in a small way, she was relieved. Hensley didn't want to fire her, at least.

"Calm down," he sniffed. "Please." He seemed to understand he needed to apologize, but refused to. Always such a dick. "Now, seriously," he said, "we don't want to lose you. It's not even midterms. It wouldn't be fair to the students, nor to us. I'm already teaching five classes. I literally don't have time for any more. We just want to know what's going on with you, that's all."

"You know what's going on with me, Walt. I've told you everything, which I kinda wish I hadn't. You sorta have me over a barrel here."

Hensley stood, and wrapped up the second half of his sandwich.

"Look, the only one who's causing any ruckus is you, Hetta. We like you. Please, just do what you said you would, what you signed the contract for, and there's no problem. Go easy on the kids. Give them a break. I'm sure plenty of people gave you one. And I'll talk to the Tanner kid again, if I need to. Nobody takes your class who isn't actually, you know, *enrolled*. Understood?"

There was a long, loaded silence. Finally, Hetta nodded.

Hensley looked down at her uneaten sandwich. "Hey, if you're not gonna touch that, I'll take it. We'll feed it to the puppies."

***

Calm down. The words burned her on the way home. *Calm down.* The gall of that man. She made the hour drive over the mountain in her little Ford Fiesta that threatened to break down at any moment, her fingers squeezing the life out of the steering wheel. She spat out the window.

That night over dinner, a cold chicken salad she'd picked at three nights in a row now, the ash heap of Hetta's pride still smoldered. The nerve of that soft, pasty, pampered man. She wanted to quit in a huff, just to prove a point, but she couldn't, she needed the money. She was always just one paycheck away from homelessness, and Hensley knew it. He was using it against her, he got a sick satisfaction out of it, of course he did.

The real question was what to do about it. How to spin it to her advantage. There weren't that many options. The school wouldn't budge on certain things, the endless hoops of rules and regs, and there were deans and provosts and CAOs and other faceless agents of the academy, those shapeless older men and women whom she passed in the hallway, their sensible khakis rubbing between their swollen thighs like nervous whispers. They were afraid, too. No, the only things that budged around here were actual people, and when she studied it from every angle, the only person, the only budgeable person who mattered, was Hensley himself. He was not only the head of the department, but its busiest teacher. He dominated the faculty in more ways than one.

But if he were to quit or be removed somehow, the other teachers would have to cover his spot, and there would be more openings, more classes to teach, more opportunity. Hell, in a situation like that, Hetta might even be asked to *join* the faculty. If that happened, she would be on salary, she could move closer to the college, find a decent rent on a cute little place nearby. Maybe even buy a house. She could make a living for herself, and a life, not scratching out a meager subsistence working as a fucking adjunct. She would be faculty. She would be a member of the club.

Part of herself—the brave and stupid part of her that said all the things she really wanted to—spoke up: *Honey, if only Hensley were gone...* The night outside seemed to quiet itself, the world beyond the windows hushed, it seemed to close around her, to shrink down to the size of her tiny apartment. The only sound, the only vibration, was the heartbeat in her chest: *If only. Hensley. Were gone.*

That night she lay in her single bed, the one she inherited when her dad passed away—one of the only halfway-usable things he gave her— thinking this thought over and over. *If only Hensley were gone.* It would be so easy. Someone, one of the tenured faculty, would slide right into his place, and she could slide right into theirs. Like Tetris.

The problem was that Hensley wasn't old; he was only middle-aged, and strong. He ran 5Ks and played racquetball in the university gym. When Hetta watched him from her office window, the one they gave her only because she'd insisted on it, she would see him crossing the bare quad with his wife and his two impossibly blonde daughters, the older and the younger. Hensley, the proud father. Hensley, the alpha of his clan.

No, *if only Hensley were gone* wouldn't be happening any time soon.

two

THE NEXT DAY she had an appointment with Tanner. He'd requested time with her, even though they both knew it was hopeless. She genuinely felt sorry for him—local kid, methed-up family, nothing beyond a piss-warm county high school education—but in class she'd come to rely on his observations and questions, his voracious energy for film. If he'd had a half an education worth a shit, his work would run circles around the other kids. It was a goddamn shame.

She was in her office, and he came inside with a knock and a solemn nod and holding his ever present Big Gulp cup—he seemed to have it with him everywhere, always half-full of room-temp sweet tea—but at first he didn't say anything. He knew his time was up. He was wiry and dark, with a bowl-cut straight across his forehead. For some reason, his body hadn't fully developed—maybe he'd been a preemie or something—so his frame was small and scraggy, about the size of a thirteen-year-old boy. He exuded poverty, he oozed Appalachian deprival, he was like a Walker Evans photograph, but he wasn't stupid. He knew every filmmaker of note—from Max Ophuls to Robert Altman to Bela Tarr and beyond. He was a walking encyclopedia.

"I don't care," he offered as he sat down. This surprised her. It was her impression that he did care, very much. "I'm not here to study movies, anyway. I wanna *make* movies."

"Yeah, well." If only Hensley were gone, she could design her own course—*Filmmaking for Non-Majors*. It would cover her own heroes, artists like Chantal Ackerman and Agnès Varda, not the rich white dudes the academy was always propping up. And she would let kids from the community come, let the local kids have a chance. It would be completely egalitarian. She could see it—her class full to bursting as she enlightened the locals about the great undervalued filmmakers, and then sent them out to be great filmmakers themselves. She would give them a voice of their own, a new rural art-film movement, the Appalachian New Wave, the voice of the people would be the people themselves. "I wish you could, too," she said.

"Then let's fuckin' do it!" Tanner's voice was shrill, it did this when he was excited or upset. He took a calming sip from his Big Gulp. It was the size of his head. "All the equipment sitting in storage, for chrissakes."

It was true. When the college had talked about starting its own film and media department, the Sony corporation had donated a huge camera—$60,000 worth of camera, 6K resolution and big as a bazooka—to the department. They were trying to claim the market, so they literally gave them away to film schools large and small around the country. And now theirs sat boxed up in their back storeroom in the dark, gathering dust. No one but Mickey Moffett, the department tech, had ever even turned it on.

Hetta glanced out her office window. The quad was mostly empty. "It's disappointing," she admitted. She told him about what Hensley had said, and also her own frustrations about the whole thing. She told him about how the pecking order went, and if only Hensley were gone, she would likely have a little more say-so around the place. "But there's nothing I can do about it." *Nothing*, she thought, *unless something happens to Herr Hensley.*

She glanced at the clock. Ten minutes until her next class, and she had yet to prepare what she was gonna talk about. "But hey, look, I'll do my best. For now, lay low. We'll talk when we can."

Tanner stood up. "So I'm really not allowed in there? I came all the way out."

"Not today. But we'll do what we can."

Tanner sipped from his Big Gulp and closed the door behind him.

And sure enough, the class wasn't the same. The rest of the kids sat there slack-faced while Hetta talked about *mise en scene* and the auteur theory. They weren't interested. The few that might have been didn't seem to get it. Tanner's empty chair stared at her, somehow as slack as the rest of them.

***

hey look at this

The text dinged on her phone just before midnight. It was Tanner. She was in bed rereading Deleuze when it came in. When no further message followed, she sent a reply: *And…?*

Five or so minutes later, the reply came. *you know that movie the ring? The one where it kills if you wach a film*

Hetta glanced at the clock. It was late, too late for this kind of thing. *So what?* she wrote.

The reply shocked her. *i have an idea*

For a long time, Hetta stared at the words. The fuck? That came out of nowhere. She wrote back, *All right, settle down, Beavis.*

He didn't respond. She turned off her phone, then the light, and lay sleepless in the dark for another two hours.

***

When she woke the next morning and turned on her phone, there was another message.

check it out

There was a link. She clicked it, but the browser on her phone took her only to a blank page. In the URL, the site was named *Mightyblur*, whatever that was, but there was nothing there, just a white screen. She put down her phone and went to take a shower. She had to get on the road.

Later, in her office, she tried the link again, to no avail. Just a blank white screen.

After class, when she tried it on her desktop computer, the same white screen came up, but here she noticed it seemed to scroll down for forever. Way, way down at the bottom, nearly the same color as the background, was a single dot. A period, or a pixel. But her cursor turned into a little hand when she hovered over it. It was a link. Puzzled, she clicked.

It loaded another page. *Voodoo Glam*, this one said, and displayed a solid wall of HTML links in a primitive ASCII layout, like something from 1993. *DISMEMBERMENT* was the title of one of them. *STALKING YOUR PREY* was another. *ANIMAL ANATOMY* and *EMBALMING* were others. At the top of the page, in a blinking red font, were the words *BE CAREFUL. Use a VPN or risk getting caught!!!*

Suddenly worried—she was using state-funded campus equipment, after all, she could lose her job visiting the wrong site—Hetta closed the browser. Then she opened a private browser, she'd pirated old film noirs from time to time, and knew how this stuff worked, and retraced her steps back to Voodoo Glam. When she clicked several of the links, she saw most of the forums on the page had their own sub-forums—*Beheadings, Urban Terrorism, Industrial Accidents, Cadavery.* Just looking at it made her feel scummy. *Suicides.* Toward the bottom there was one that said *So Sick o' You.*

She clicked that one. A sub-sub-forum loaded. *Methods of Liquidation,* this one said. *Freezings, Crushings, Drownings, Accidents,* and *Poisons* were some of the headers. There were a surprising number of ways to off someone. But halfway down the second page, something odd even for this site caught her eye: *8:59:29,* it said, with a little blinking star-badge that warned *watch your step!*

Hetta couldn't resist. She clicked, and it loaded a long page of text, no paragraphs, just a brick of Courier, black on white. It was an essay, evidently by a user named *williewaster456.*

For the next hour, she read what *williewaster456,* whoever he was, had to say, and didn't stir until one of her students came and timidly knocked on the door and told her she was late for a meeting.

***

"What the *fuck,* Tanner?" Hetta said.

They were sitting in a sleepy bar called Nuzzlurz. It was the tiny college town's only beer joint, but for some inexplicable reason the decor was aggressively old-fashioned, as though somebody's grandma had futzed it together. Doilies lay on every table, with lumpy couches and antique end tables that leaned worryingly when you put a beer on them. None of the college kids ever seemed to hang out there, and Hetta often wondered how Nuzzlurz stayed afloat. Aside from the skinny girl scrolling on her phone behind the counter, they had the place to themselves.

"Yeah, wild, huh? There's all kinds of sick shit on there."

"How do you know about this stuff?"

Tanner didn't answer, he only pressed his lips, like the question itself was off limits. For the first time in a long while, Hetta looked at him afresh, considered the scarecrow frame of his body as an item of interest. His features were oddly undercooked. He hit his rescue inhaler almost as constantly as he sipped from the straw of his Big Gulp. But somehow he made up for this frailty with ample attitude—his sleeves and the collar of his shirt half-hid multiple amateurish but elaborate tats, by now as green and smeared as any old Vietnam vet's. Hetta guessed he spent a lot of his free time playing video games with his bros. Aside from his delicate physical state and his savant knowledge of film classics, Tanner seemed like your usual run-of-the-mill small-town bucket of testosterone. She was surprised they got along so well.

But that site—geez, that site. If the internet was a cesspool, then Voodoo Glam was the sludge at the very bottom. Beyond all the pedestrian but undeniably effective strategies for revenge was a section for occult rituals, most of them from centuries ago, with abstruse, almost incomprehensible texts and extended footnotes. The transcriptions had the intricate and inaccessible feel of authenticity. She'd read a lot of crazy crap in her time, but these instructions were intimidating. "Seriously, how do you know this?" she said.

"I read. I look around. I know people." He shrugged. "Did you look at all of them?"

"I looked at enough."

"Did you find the one I was hoping you would?"

"The film project? Nine Fifteen or whatever it was called?"

Tanner's eyes were half-lidded, but not from any beer or drugs. He was smug, proud of himself, proud of this score. The industrial refrigerator behind them kicked on right then, and Tanner mumbled something she didn't catch. Hetta shook her head. "*Andras*," Tanner repeated. He rolled the "r," like Spanish. "He's a demon."

"A *demon*?" Even though the empty space of Nuzzlurz couldn't get any brighter—it faced west, and the sun burned through the place every afternoon—it had somehow taken on a deeper, more desolate vibe. She stole a look over at the girl behind the counter. Still absorbed in her phone. "From what?"

"Hey, I know things too." Tanner sipped on the straw of his Big Gulp, and Hetta watched the brown liquid go up and up and into Tanner's mouth. "But maybe he can help us." He looked at Hetta. He was smiling, but his eyes weren't.

"*Andras*," Hetta said to herself. It sounded so silly. *He*. Were demons bound by gender? Did demons actually *exist*? They were so blasé, so yesterday, so 1970's. "I didn't really understand," she confessed, "what that article was supposed to be."

That article. Hetta had stayed up all night reading and rereading it. Though *williewaster456* never came out and directly said so, it was about how to create a movie that would kill whoever was unfortunate enough to watch it. And then their soul would be sent to Hell and damnation everlasting. Exactly how, the text never specified.

"First, you go insane," Tanner explained with a ghastly relish. "*Then* you die. You kill yourself, or do something drastic. Andras is supposedly the one arranging everything. He's like the host of the party."

"But…people killing themselves? Just from a video?"

"To be honest, yeah, I'm not really into the whole death part, either. I just want to know if it works."

"It got pretty specific. Frame rates and stuff like that." The frame rate part had particularly impressed her. It was, in fact, the reason this plan had appealed to her in the first place.

"How so?"

"Well, I covered this in class the other day when you were gone. American video isn't exactly thirty frames, it's more like 29.97. That last frame never gets completed. It's a fragment of a frame, a decimal point, a percentage, which throws everything off."

"So?"

Hetta sipped from her beer. "Because of that discrepancy, you have a case where video time and real time don't match up. There's a skip." That skip was where the true enigma lay: it defied logic, it took the work into a place beyond linear time and into…where? "And inside that skip, those partial forgotten frames," she said, "that's where the trouble lives."

Tanner shook his head in admiration. "That's dope."

"Most of the ritual seems laid out right there."

"Most of it?" It was Tanner's turn to glance at the girl behind the counter, and Hetta saw a mild lust percolating in his gaze. The girl was cute, and she looked sweet, too, a nice girl, but there was a canyon of privilege and distance between the students and the townies. Tanner, poor guy, didn't stand a chance.

"We're lacking the right equipment," Hetta explained. "We don't have it."

"We've got the whole storeroom full of video crap. Mickey Moffett showed it to me."

We. There was no *we.* Tanner wasn't part of the curriculum, he never really was, but she let it slide. "Yeah, but it says we don't need that. We need a VHS camera. Specifically, one made by Hitachi. Specifically in 1985. That's what the instructions said."

Tanner frowned. He wasn't even born in 1985. "But where would you get a camera like that?"

"I dunno. eBay, maybe?"

"Good fuckin' luck with that. Nobody keeps cameras around like that anymore."

They both went silent at this. Film technology had moved so fast there was a new camera, a new format, a new higher resolution every year. In film and video terms, 1985 was pre-history.

Outside, a panel truck rumbled by, and for a moment the sun was gone and they sat in shadow, night suddenly dropped upon the cafe. Then the truck passed and the sun was back.

Tanner wiped his mouth with a napkin, balled it up, and shot it like a basketball at a nearby trash can. He missed. "I dunno," he said. "Now I wish I hadn't sent it your way. Who knows if it's even real? Maybe you should let it go."

***

Hetta didn't let it go. For the next two days she scoured the web, looking for a Hitachi VM-200A, which would take a full-sized VHS tape and play it at the three-hour speed, like *williewaster456* specified. She found several online, but none that actually worked. Most were paperweights, their owners said, good now only for parts or props.

But then, on the third day, someone uploaded a new listing. *Hitachi VHS Camcorder Model VM-200A,* it said. *Tested, Works, Needs New Belt. Is in okay condition, but needs a new belt to fully eject tape deck. See Pics."*

And there was the camera—a black, boxy thing, all hard angles, a handle on top, and a lens poking out like a stubby snout. Somehow in a glance it evoked an entire world—the 80's in all its naïve and artificial charm. The plastic body was faded and mottled, maybe with even a little mold, but it came with a case and a huge battery that plugged into any outlet. It was a beast. Best of all, it was under $30—even at her meager adjunct pay, she could afford it. And ejecting the tape wouldn't be a problem. She'd most likely only need to do that once.

She printed up *williewaster456*'s instructions, and read over them again in her office. *This is a tride and true method,* it said. *But Utmoust Caution should be used u must follw my instrctions exalty, but what else is new haha*

Apparently, the movie would need to be exactly 8:59:29 long. Eight minutes, fifty-nine seconds, and 29 frames. Imbedded in those incomplete frames, that .97 every second, would somehow be the influence of one of the Great Earls of Hell. *Most likely it will be Andras,* the instructions said, and that was followed by a quote.

> *The Dutch demonologist Johannes Weir, in his Pseudomonarchia Daemonum, says of Andras: Andras is a great marquesse, and seemes in an angels shape with a head like a blacke night raven, riding upon a blacke and a verie strong woolfe, flourishing with a sharpe sword in his hand, he can kill the maister, the servant, and all assistants, he is the author of discords, and ruleth thirtie legions.*

A head like a black raven, riding upon a black wolf? Please. Hetta wanted to roll her eyes. She was almost embarrassed for him.

And there were the instructions. *For our purposes,* the author wrote— this wasn't *williewaster456,* because there were hardly any typos—*only the final, fractional frames of each second will be used, and a specific amount of them must be accumulated. And because the video is interlaced, two partial fields endlessly intertwined, this allows the ghost, if you will, to slip between the cracks and enter the machine.*

Huh. A short film. Hetta would have to make a short film. Something that Hensley would watch all the way through. It had to be compelling. It had to be worth watching. It had to be *good.*

Her stomach clenched. Here was the test. Could she do it? For so many years she'd carried around an attitude that she had been a latent talent, a natural virtuoso denied her moment in the spotlight. But now here she was, exploring a revenge strategy on a man who had insulted her, who had accused her of not being able to swim with the big boys, while privately sweating the man's point. Maybe Hensley was right? Maybe she did kinda, you know, suck?

She laughed aloud, an unfamiliar choppy bark that sounded strange in her empty apartment. How was she gonna get it done? There would be lights. Audio. Sets. Movies were an undertaking. Practically any production required a crew. PAs, sound people, gaffers, assistant directors, script supervisors. She would have none of that. It would be her, and her alone.

Well, there were always her students. She could maybe create an extra-credit project, a weekend project, give them a chance to make up for all those crappy grades she gave them.

Yeah, no. That wouldn't work. Most of them were idiots who had no idea what to do on a film set. The only camera they'd ever held was in their phone. They recorded their silly little social media posts in portrait mode. Really, they would just be in the way. And besides, if it turned out okay, if the film did what she wanted it to, Hetta didn't want them implicated. This was a task done alone or not at all.

But that was impossible. There was no way she could do it by herself.

Hetta looked at her phone, sitting on its face on the table. She always turned it face down, so no weird hackers or spyware could watch her. After a few minutes, she picked it up. She wrote, *Hey Tanner, let's talk.*

three

A FILM BY. A film by Hetta Salter. A short film by Hetta D. Salter. A Hetta D. Salter Film. A Hetta D. Salter Production.
She was starting to get used to it. It didn't sound so weird anymore. For so many years, particularly in college, she'd expected to make a film. It seemed so easy, other people did it, no problem. But then one thing after another had come up—debt, a parent's illness, a pet's illness, a pricey car repair. The idea slipped away from her, receded into the cluttered distance where everything else she'd dreamed about seemed to dwell. The further she reached, the more it retreated. Eventually, without even knowing it, she'd given up.

But now, after all this time judging and criticizing others' work, she would get the chance to offer some of her own. It was scarier than it sounded. Terrifying, actually, and she wasn't even talking about the "demon" part. Hetta sat down at her kitchen table with a pen and a piece of paper. What kind of movie would she make? A drama? Eh, maybe, maybe not. That seemed kind of boring. Old white people talking about old white people stuff. She was no fan of modern cinema, with its comic book movies and endless spectacle, but she suspected that even people of her age and predilections had lost most of their interest in the quiet black and white introspections of Bergman and Truffaut.

Better to make it more, you know, contemporary.

So, a comedy? Ehh. Comedy was hard, nowhere nearly as effortless as it looked. In comedy, falling on your face was almost assured, when you tried to be funny and failed, your movie was DOA. Nothing's scarier than a comedy when no one's laughing. She'd seen it happen so many times. Better to leave comedy to the masters.

Maybe something abstract, then, like Brakhage, all squiggly lines and muted colors going this way and that. Geometries and symbols, scritches and scratches and architectural details superimposed on the faces of classical statues.

Nah. When Hetta let herself admit it, she hated Brakhage's work. It was so old-school as to be primeval, playing with concepts and questions that belonged to a man's view of the 20th century, not a woman's of the 21st. Plus Brakhage often used the physical medium itself, painting on the actual film print. She would be using good old VHS—and early VHS at that—and would have no way to make any physical alterations.

Maybe she could adapt a short story, something written by someone else? Hey, Kubrick did it, why not her? Still valid, right?

Ixnay on that. Her gut told her that was the wrong approach. She was supposedly sending this guy to Hell, so the least she could do was to come up with her own goddamn script. She could give him that much. And anyway, who had the money for option fees? She'd helped hundreds of young people learn the craft of screenwriting. Surely she could do it herself?

Yep, she was gonna to have to make a film of her own, her very own, built solely from her own interests. But what would that look like, what was she interested in? It wasn't a question she had the luxury of asking herself very often. What excited her? She tapped her pen on the paper and shifted in her chair. She was kind of a World War II buff. Nazis, the Allies, North Africa, machine guns and combat greens and tanks in the desert. She had half a dozen books about it lying around the house.

Yeah, but that was impossible. A film like that would have period cars and props and costumes and locations. And on her budget, that wouldn't work.

Maybe…a film noir? Stairways and fedoras and femme fatales. Shadows broken by the bright stutter of neon signs. Handguns and hotels and alleyways.

Nah. Fun, but done. And hard to pull off, anyway. You still needed locations and lights and costumes. She couldn't afford it.

She looked around at her apartment. Shabby couch, tiny TV, battered kitchen table. Cinderblock bookcases crammed with dog-eared paperbacks. This place wasn't awful. It was funky but it had a vibe, an atmosphere. Could she film here? A little cramped, not really cinematic, but the morning light coming in was nice, it was bright enough and the sun fell along the floor in fun little patterns and coruscations.

She leaned back in her chair. It creaked under her weight. She'd had this furniture since college. By now she'd supposed she would have had new furniture, a whole set of it, but circumstances didn't seem to allow for that. Or maybe *she* didn't allow for that. It was just her, alone, she wasn't married, she'd never been married. No one had ever stuck around except her ex-boyfriend Robby, and now he was gone, too. Too angry, Robby had said, too insecure, too needy. *Too too too*—there was always some reason the phone stopped ringing. By the end of the day, the excuses were all the same: no one liked Hetta. No one liked her attitude, no one liked her past, and no one liked her future.

That was okay. She didn't like them either.

All right, what about a documentary? She could film out on the streets, cars buzzing this way and that, crowds of people strolling the sidewalks. She could go to some big city financial district and get shots of taxis and flying helicopters reflected in glass buildings as they passed. Maybe some interviews with important people, maybe with her putting them on the spot. A gotcha exposé piece—*Hetta versus the Man*.

She took a deep breath. No, that'd been done to death. She'd seen it a thousand times, and mainly it meant the filmmaker was out of ideas, or never had any to begin with. Just hit the red button and see what happens, that was what documentaries were, the last refuge of the artless filmmaker. No, if she was going to put a demon's image in her film—Andras, a Marquis of Hell, no less—she would need to come up with a movie that was truly worthy of him.

Okay then, back to the dramas. Resnais, Bergman, Ozu, Bresson. All masters at capturing the landscape of the human face. A quiet drama. A single conversation, maybe, between two people. Then the conversation turns, dramatically so, like *My Dinner with Andre*. That would be doable. Set in her apartment. Like something from the French New Wave.

With a measure of new optimism, she uncapped her pen. On the paper, she wrote, *MAN* and *WOMAN*. After a moment's pause, she kept going.

Man comes in the door. MAN: Hi.

Woman sitting at the table. WOMAN: Hello.

Man takes off his hat. MAN: Hello, how are you?

Woman smiles. WOMAN: I'm fine, how are you?

Man puts his hat on the coat tree. MAN: I am fine.

No no no. Hetta ripped the page from the notebook and balled it up and dropped it on the floor. Terrible. Like a screenplay written by a bot. She had no idea where it would go, where this man and woman would lead her.

She looked down at the new blank page. It was so big, so white.

Maybe the man comes in, and the woman slaps him.

No, too melodramatic. Maybe she's crying.

No, too sexist and clichéd. Wait—maybe *he's* crying, and then *he* slaps her?

Yeah, no, Hetta didn't do male-on-female violence. Too much of that already in the world.

Damn. She sucked on her lip. Tapped the pen on the paper. Drew a squiggly line. Then another squiggly line underneath that. Took another deep breath.

She glanced into the kitchen, where the last heel of the rye bread sat, getting old. She needed to eat that up before it went bad. Lunch. She needed lunch.

***

Hey. You around?

She was lying in bed looking at her phone, thinking how she would say it. But in less than ten seconds, he wrote back.

yep whats up

What are your ideas about a short film? Making a short film, I mean. I need something we can shoot that will work on no budget. Video only. What are your thoughts?

that's easy a fucking horror movie

Horror, hm. Hetta hadn't seriously considered that one. For years, her bedside lamp had thrown odd shadows on the ceiling, like a man reaching. She'd seen it for half a decade, it reminded her every night of some German expressionist film or other. A horror film. Well. You could film horror for cheap—fake blood was nothing, she could even make it herself. A couple of actors, a knife or a chainsaw, *slice buzz whoosh splat*, she'd be done. And you could sometimes tackle a serious theme or two, besides.

Not terrible, she wrote back. *How would we do it?*

The answer came back immediately: *easy we'll do a snuff film torture porn tie a girl to a chair and make her scream*

Uh, no. Hetta was desperate, but she wasn't that desperate. *Nah,* she wrote. *We need a story, and a script. And actors. We need a movie.*

i can act, the reply said. *my mom used to make me do summer theater and i've done movie gore I can do any fx you want*

Tanner, *acting?* Now that was a bizarre notion. Hetta couldn't think of anything she'd rather see less than Tanner's bony body onscreen, with his hairy shins poking out from his basketball shorts like the wooden handles on a corndog. She studied the shadows on the ceiling. But tension, blood, gore. That was good. That was very good.

Nah, I need you behind the camera, she wrote. *But let's talk.*

four

TANNER CAME OVER the next morning. Oddly, he'd paled his face with white makeup, and sported vampire teeth and a long black cape with what looked like a crimson satin lining. A little dribble of pink blood was drawn down on one side of his mouth.

"Um, hi," Hetta said, surveying him as he stood in the doorway. "What are you doing?"

"Just gettin' in the mood, man," Tanner said.

"Well, all right, then." Hetta stood aside to let him in.

Tanner lugged in a book bag, which he threw down with a thump on the kitchen table. "I've already got a plan," he announced. "One room, two actors, nine minutes. Right?"

"Something like that."

"How 'bout this." He turned grandly to face Hetta, and she saw how focused he was. A distant glory burned in his eyes, a bright self-satisfaction at the depths of his own creative powers. He was high on his own supply. "Hear me out. A man and a woman. In conversation. Sitting on the couch. You think they're just two normal people on a date. But then the man is slowly revealed to be..." He took a moment, to let the anticipation grow. "A mummy."

Hetta sat down at the table. "A mummy?" Tanner nodded. "Wouldn't we, like, see the bandages and the wraps?"

Tanner sat, too. "Not really. Maybe this mummy doesn't have wraps. Maybe this mummy is different. A modern mummy." He took his vampire teeth out and put them, Hetta noticed with distaste, on the kitchen table. "As a matter of fact, you can call it *The Modern Mummy*."

"Eh, then how do we know it's a mummy? Mummies are all about the wraps. I dunno."

Tanner was undeterred. "Well, okay. Plan B, then. The man is slowly

POLLY SCHATTEL

unmasked to be a"—he moved his hands in a slow reveal—"a *werewolf.*"

Unmasked. Werewolves have masks? Hetta tried not to show her irritation. She was starting to regret asking him for help. Maybe even starting to regret this whole thing, this whole idiotic project. Kill Hensley, and send him to *Hell?* Jesus, talk about overreacting. But then she looked around her shabby apartment, and saw Hensley's bland sanctimonious face in her head, and the need for redress became real again.

"I dunno," she said. "It sounds hokey." But still, the one-room conversation idea, it had possibility. It was like a Rohmer film, pure conversation. But a horror version.

"What about a vampire," she said, looking at his cape. "Two people talking, and he—or *she*, actually, I like *she* better—*she* is slowly revealed to be a vampire."

"Okay," Tanner said defensively. His breath whistled loudly in and out of his nose. "Not my first choice, but, you know. Okay."

For the next hour they sat at the table and brainstormed a scenario. A woman knocks, comes to a man's apartment, invited by the man, of course. They sit and have a cup of coffee—or whiskey, yeah, they have whiskey—and talk. Things are mundane, but slowly get more tense, in a subtle way. "Clues are dropped," Hetta said, "hints are given, patterns emerge. You think it's gonna switch, and the monster will be revealed to be the man. But at the end it's the *woman,* see, who bites the *man.* It was her all along. The surprise is that—hey, there's no surprise." Hetta pumped her fist. "And...roll credits."

Tanner was silent, thinking it all through. "Mmm, I can live with that," he said finally. He sat back and picked at the woodgrain in the tabletop. With his pale makeup, he looked tired. Hetta could see what he would look like as a dead man in his coffin. "I kinda dig it, now that we're talking about it. I see it. A little slow maybe, so we need blood. Lots of blood."

"I dunno, the absence of blood is what's cool about it. Don't you see? People will *expect* blood. That way we surprise them. That's the trick." Plus, she knew Hensley hated schlock horror and would never watch anything even close to it. He forbade his students to make horror projects in their senior-class short films. No doubt there was a negative experience somewhere in the past—cheesy student horror movies, mountain-born Pentecostal community, parents complaining to the goddamn *provost*—and he'd said no more horror. And anyway, Hetta reminded herself to keep her eyes on the prize—it wasn't really about the movie, after all, it was about her getting Hensley to watch the thing all the way through. It was about getting herself a place on the faculty. Maybe even tenure track. *If only Hensley were gone.* It was her mantra now.

"And anyway," she said, "you don't buy someone a present you want, you buy the present they want."

"Whatever *that* means," Tanner said with a defeated tone.

***

By the weekend, she had a full script. The man, unnamed, invites the woman inside. The woman, also unnamed, sits, and they talk. The conversation is banal, purposefully so, lulling you, boring you, and then just before the credits, right when you expect a huge reveal, it *doesn't* switch, the surprise is that there's no surprise, the woman is indeed the vampire, it was her all along and she ambushes the man and bites him on the neck. *The End.*

"But nothing *happens*," Tanner complained when he read it.

"That's the point," Hetta said, feeling a little defensive, and also resentful that even now, even here, at the dawn of her first film, her first true expression of self, she was having to justify her decisions to another clueless white male. Tanner must have seen the look in her eyes, because he kept his mouth shut.

Hetta put a notice in the local alternative weekly calling for two actors. By the end of the first day her mailbox downstairs was overwhelmed. By the end of the second day, she called the paper and cancelled the ad because the postman was grumbling about having to haul the load of mail up the stairs and drop it at her door. There were piles of envelopes and boxes, videotapes and headshots, web links and YouTube reels. Some of the actors had a surprising amount of experience—other films, TV shows, extensive theater work. Some were children, obviously not right at all for the part, their desperate mothers no doubt sent the poor kids to all the casting calls. But almost every one of the actors was weirdly, eerily appealing—eyes bright and grinning, their teeth perfect, their skin flawless. They *were* vampires, they wanted to suck the life out of her, out of her production, with their hunger to be noticed, to be loved, to be famous. Hetta hated every one of them.

She chose the two she did based more on their looks than on experience. She went with her gut: the woman was tall and beautiful, with a ski-slope nose and a waist-length downpour of smooth black hair. The man was more vanilla, just a dude, a pasty white putz with a cowering hairline and the beginnings of jowls. Midlife blandness was taking over him like a tree being swallowed by kudzu.

Hetta scheduled the shoot for Saturday night, as soon as the sun went down. She and Tanner spent the day getting her apartment ready. Set dressing, arranging the table lamps just right—*practicals*, Tanner kept calling them—and blocking out the shots and angles. Finally, as the actors arrived and came inside, already in costume and chatting endlessly about themselves, Hetta readied the final details. She set the camera's aperture just a tad underexposed, right where the Hitachi liked it. She'd never been a people person, but technical details were no problem; she had an engineer's brain and could practically write camera manuals herself. Maybe she should've done that, she thought, looking around at her cramped apartment with the lousy camera and the chintzy tripod. It certainly paid better.

The shoot itself was nothing, it was as surprisingly unsurprising as the script itself. The woman, Reeta, was self-obsessed and testy, and the man, Bob, was as tedious as expected. But Hetta liked that, actually, she appreciated how it contributed to the point of the piece in an odd but very real way. She could *feel* it in her gut. The main problem was that Bob had an impression he was in a David Lynch film, and overplayed the weirdness of everything. Directing him, Hetta had to pull him back and remind him that he was the normal one. "So all the while you think you're outsmarting her, but she's the one outsmarting *you*," Hetta said, flipping her hand over like a magician revealing a card. "See, it turns."

"But it doesn't turn," Bob said. "We think she's the vampire, and then she is the vampire." He kept pronouncing it like *wampeer*. "She gets me in the end."

"Right, but *that's* the turn," Hetta said. "Don't you see?" Bob only blinked, he didn't see. "All right, let's go again," she said.

In addition to everything else, Tanner ran sound. He didn't have a boom pole, so he held the mic out at arm's length, just out of frame, and did the best he could. Every so often he would call *"PLANE!"* way too loud in the room and pause everyone. Hetta wondered if he was also trying to notify the neighbors. She didn't complain, though—Tanner was working hard, he was also handling the edit, he'd torrented all the software and was pretty good at it, too, from what she'd seen. He'd sent her a few YouTube movies he'd made of him and his little brother running around the county dump behind their house. The movies weren't completely terrible.

five

OR MOST OF the next week, Hetta waited for Tanner to deliver the rough cut. Her nerves were beginning to fray as she suffered through more tedious classes, more dreary afternoons in her barren office, staring out at the dirt quad beyond and listening to Hensley's irksome honk of a voice coming and going outside her closed door. It was like a city train you didn't want to catch but had to anyway. She consoled herself with thinking about the short movie. What she had seen during filming had looked okay. She closed her eyes and let the shots unspool in her head again—the light rippling up and down Reeta's long black hair, the over-the-shoulder shot that highlighted the ripe fleshiness of Bob's neck. The way the corners of her apartment fell into perfect parabolas of shadow. It really *was* cinematic.

In her head, the title had changed several times. It had started out being called *The Conversation*, but Coppola, damn him, had already claimed that one. When Tanner finally came over to her office with the rough cut on a thumb drive, she was calling it *The Lurker on the Loveseat*. He told her he'd had to break the camera's cassette compartment to get the tape out—*no reshoots, girl*, Hetta noted grimly—and had digitized the VHS, and cut it all together. With more than a little trepidation, Hetta dragged the icon—named only *mymovie.mov*—from the thumb drive to her own computer.

But just as she was about to click the link, a terrible thought appeared, like a pimple on her brain—what if the complicated time coordinations of the video had somehow gotten corrupted in the transfer from tape to computer? Digital video and analog video didn't operate the same, the particulars weren't the same, what had been 29.97 frames a second was now…what? Who could say? Whatever rate Tanner had captured the video into the hard drive, she supposed.

Captured. Hetta's brain jerked to a halt on that word. Unfortunate choice of terminology.

"Look, dude," she said as he pulled up the chair across from her desk. "Are you sure this is right? Twenty nine point nine seven, right?"

"Of course. Exactly as you asked." Tanner seemed hurt. "Just watch, *shhhh.*"

On the screen there was a white flash, and then a countdown. *Tan-Man Moviepictures,* it said. And finally, the image faded up.

As the video played, a sense of relief passed over her—it was better than expected. The lighting wasn't bad, the flesh tones radiated, the chiaroscuro of the faces rolled off nicely into shadow. The VHS images had a nasty, low-fi feeling, like a patina covering the screen, and there were the usual analog artifacts—tape dropouts, glitches, static, and in the dark corners of the screen, blocky chunks of shadow flickering like black fire. Pixels burned and died out, tracking came and went, and bands of color and noise roamed up and down the screen, but apparently that was all normal, all part of the VHS plan. At least *williewaster456* said so.

Other than that, it looked good. Reeta was backlit in the shots at the door, giving her an almost spectral corona. But Hetta noticed the actress was weirdly stiff—it hadn't felt that way that night in the room, she'd come off as elegant, but here her performance felt too small, too normal, too flat—under-the-top, rather than over. Bob, though, when he spoke for the first time, a funny feeling passed through Hetta. There was a sense of absence, of herself being yanked into the moment, into the reality of the story. It surprised her: Bob was nailing it. What had felt too weird in the room that night played wonderfully on camera. He had all the banal, jowly menace of a neighborhood serial killer. In contrast to what it had felt like on the shoot, his performance came off as natural, interesting, convincing. It *worked.* And thus when the narrative flip came—or, rather, *didn't* come—it was surprising and scary, just as she'd hoped.

"Holy shit, Tanner," Hetta said when the whole thing had played through. She sat back. "It's fine. The edits, they're not quite there yet. But shit. Overall it's not bad."

Tanner started bouncing up and down in his chair, his thin arms straining. *"Yih-yeah,"* he said, and kicked the desk.

***

Within a week they had it—the final cut. It was exactly eight minutes, fifty-nine seconds and twenty-nine frames long. *williewaster456* would be proud. And despite herself, Hetta resisted being more precious about the whole thing—it was her first completed short film, after all, the groundwork of her legacy, a minor but vital part of what she would be remembered for forever. But this video had a different purpose: ultimately it didn't matter if it was good or not, Hensley just had to watch it. Of course, for her own personal artistic rectitude she was making it good, she was a perfectionist, of course she was. But even then she recognized there came a point of diminishing returns. When it was finished, the movie would be watched only once, and by only one person. So after four nights of intense back and forth—Tanner drove the edit over and they watched it together, with Hetta taking notes—she pronounced them ready for the next phase. It was time for the ritual.

This was the hard part. It was an all-day affair, and it required several random but crucial elements—the usual bells, books, and candles, but also odd things like ferret fur, thatches of mayweed and nettle, a silver dagger, and a tufa whetstone. And she would need to recite a shit-ton of language, mostly in Latin. Hetta had taken Latin for a semester in eighth grade, but by the end of that summer it had all evaporated as quickly as rain on a summer sidewalk.

She still didn't know what to think of Andras. What did he get out of it? The reference materials said his primary purpose was to sow discord among mortals, which sounded almost too perfect. The instructions warned it was distressingly easy to get the tiniest detail wrong, to create a scenario where Andras would harm the conjurer, rather than do their bidding. *That will not be me*, Hetta promised herself, and went back to studying the verses. Her journalist days had trained her, back then she was paid a pittance—always a pittance, she'd never earned anything but—to learn the complexities of something very serious very quickly. She was good at it. With a week's research she could conduct reasonable interviews about dam engineering, or arson investigations, or NASA observatories, and write articles that were remarkably informed. Of course, all that knowledge went as quickly as it came: like her Latin, it dissipated in weeks, but she could do it.

For most of a month they waited for everything to come in. EBay had changed the world, maybe not for the better, but hey—if you needed the severed hind feet of a Pakistani leopard gecko, you could get them. At the college, the semester ground on. Confounded faces looking back at her like sponges with eyes, faces that knew everything about fraternities and football, but nothing of Fellini. And the invocation ritual itself felt slightly ridiculous, like something out of a cheesy TV commercial, and not even a good bad one.

The ritual required that they project the movie on one of her walls at the precise 29.97 frames per second while the incantations were being recited. That meant Tanner needed to find a projector that allowed for that frame rate—time-wise, it had to be consistent, every step of the way. Tanner searched online for just the right projector, and the various cables and couplers and adapters, and cobbled together a way to make it happen. In her sweltering parked car outside a Taco Bell, Hetta gnawed a bean burrito and grimly studied the receipts he'd handed over. This whole thing was costing her a pretty penny, and it was taking forever. Everything seemed to be mere preparation. Nothing was *doing*.

Finally it became real when Tanner huffed everything over to her apartment in a crazy tangle of boxes and wires and doodads. With a growing sense of unease—*were they really gonna do this?*—Hetta watched him set it up. Together they pushed all the furniture against one side of the room, and they took the prints down from the wall. Hetta solemnly turned off the lights, and then with another tingle of dark wonderment—*they were gonna do this, they really were*—she hit the projector's ON button. The picture fired up. It looked fuzzy and dim, but okay.

Hetta struggled into her robe, trying not to acknowledge the vague sense of alarm that was rising like a gas leak in the room. "You ready?"

Tanner stared at his robe. It was clear he didn't want to put it on. Tanner only wore sports jerseys and basketball shorts, it was his thing, but finally he pulled it over himself. With his tiny frame, it looked as if he was wearing a dress three sizes too big. The hem dragged on the floor. "Yeah," he said dolefully.

Following the instructions, Hetta had sewn the emblem of Andras onto them, which looked to her like a measure of musical notation with a few puppet-like stick-figure people drawn on them. Two oversized arrows, at the beginning of the measure and at the end, curved inward to point, like an accusation, at the primary figure.

Tanner's stomach rumbled. They'd been fasting since the day before yesterday, and his color, even in the warm candlelight, was paler than usual. They stood in the middle of the pentacle they'd drawn on the floor, and Hetta raised the Voodoo Glam printouts close so she could see them in the half-light. The text of the introduction was surprisingly Christian, and weirdly benign in a creepy orthodox kind of way. Hetta didn't care one way or another; she cleared her throat, and in a terrible Olde English accent she exhumed from her college days of studying Chaucer, she began.

In the name of our Lord Jesus Christ, the father and the sonne and the Hollie-ghost, holie trinitie and inseparable unitie, I call upon thee, that thou maiest be my salvation and defense, and the protection of my bodie and soule, and of all my goods through the vertue of thy holie crosse, and through the vertue of thy passion, I beseech thee O Lord Jesus Christ, by the merits of thy blessed mother Marie, and of all thy saints, that thou give me grace and divine power over every wicked spirit, so as which of them soever I doo call by name, they may come by and by from everie coast, and accomplish my will, that they neither be hurtfull or fearefull unto me, but rather obedient and diligent unto me. And through thy vertue streight lie commanding them, let them fulfill my commandments, Amen.

From there it switched to Latin. The passage was quite long, actually— as she recited, Hetta could feel Tanner next to her shuffling his feet and impatiently clearing his throat. Finally, she came to the part where the visual media would be introduced. She looked at the clock. It was just shy of the ninth hour, as the instructions specified. She turned to Tanner. "Play it, please," she whispered.

On the wall, a few lines squiggled past, and then an image faded up. *What We Talk About When We Talk About Hemoglobin*, written in red font, not too obvious. It was the new title. Hetta knew Hensley was a Carver fan and would get the reference, but as usual Tanner had protested against it. And then the movie started. Hetta's first impulse was simply to watch it— she couldn't say she liked it, but it did fascinate her, emerging as it had from the dark, fairy tale forest of her own synapses—but Tanner bouncing from foot to foot next to her brought her back to the moment.

"Okay, now…*volte-face*." She and Tanner turned and stood with their backs to the image as the movie played on. She started reading, this time directly to Andras, the summoning part, the asking part. This was also in Latin—she'd used an online translator to understand what exactly was she was requesting. As she read, trickles of cold sweat dropped into her eyes and ran down her face. She'd never done anything like this before. It was one thing to talk and think about it, but another to do it. But she pushed herself through, she recited the passage with difficulty, as though wading through deep grass, and finished the appeal.

And then it was over. The movie ended. Hetta relaxed, strangely exhausted. She wiped her face and went to sit on the couch. Tanner shrugged out of his robe and turned off the projector.

"That should be that," Hetta said. "Now, just make a copy, one copy. And let's destroy the original footage."

Tanner wiped his brow and unplugged the projector, and began packing it away. "Was…uh, *he* supposed to, you know. Show up?"

"I dunno. I don't think so." Hetta stared at the carpet, letting her mind unreel. She felt almost embarrassed, humiliated, to be this raw, this vulnerable in front of someone she didn't really know that well. "How do you think it went?"

"Mmm?" Tanner looked up. He seemed distracted and uncomfortable too. "Yeah, yeah. Fine. Just a bit, you know. Intense."

Hetta got up and turned on the lights. "All right. I need a shower, and I need sleep."

six

O F COURSE SHE couldn't sleep. She was too wired, too jazzed up. She wanted to watch the movie again, but she didn't dare. It was loaded now, malignant, toxic as a poisonous flower ready to whiff out its cloud of deadly pollen. She could never watch it again.

After a couple of hours of tossing and turning, she gave up and turned on the light. The same weird shadows fell across the ceiling and the opposite wall. It really did seem like a man reaching out—there was the head, and the shoulders and the stretched-out arm. It even had fingers of a sort. Horror movies made you see nightmares everywhere, that's why Hetta preferred dramas by filmmakers like Woody Allen and Roman Polanski and people like that—there was enough trauma in the world already without subjecting yourself to random imaginary horrors. Hetta pulled her knees up to her chest. Maybe her next film would be a comedy.

She was about to turn off her light again when her phone lit up. It was Tanner.

got to go, it said. *time to see barry*

Hetta wrote back, *Haha are you still up? How many beers have you had?*

There was no reply. After a few minutes, Hetta wrote, *whats up everything okay?*

Still no reply.

Then, almost exactly nine minutes later, just one single word: *barry*

Barry. Who's Barry? she wrote back.

barry's dead

Hetta looked at her phone. Tanner was a depressed kid. Every kid was depressed, at least every one she had ever known, but Tanner was a special sort of miserable. That hardscrabble existence of his, trailers and opiates and malnutrition and full-on Appalachian hardship. You could make a pretty good documentary of his life. Hurting himself wasn't off the table; in fact, it was part of the reason she'd allowed him in the class, to boost him up and give him a little hope in his life, a glimmer of something to look forward to. But sometimes the collective weight of the young people's dread felt like a yoke around her neck. She was constantly pulling them along with no relief in sight. Not even money would fix it, really, but it would make the misery somewhat easier to bear.

Hetta hit the dial button, and listened to Tanner's phone ring. Then his message came on—a long, croaky burp, followed by the beep. She ended the call and typed *will you pick up?*

Nothing.

If you don't pick up, im coming over. tonight is not the night to fuck with me like this.

Still nothing.

Then, almost exactly nine minutes later, her phone lit up again: *barry barry me my love will you barry me*

Hetta got out of bed and started getting dressed. "Fuck fuck fuck," she said.

***

Tanner lived in a boxy apartment building in the foothills beyond the north fringe of the tiny college town. The development, which housed eight apartments or so, stood off by itself on a bare dirt ridge overlooking a rural two-lane. Hetta had dropped him off here a time or two after class, and tonight, as her car bounced and bottomed itself out on the steep, rutted road that led up to it, she cursed it even harder than she had then. Topping the hill, her lights revealed the parking lot, a gravel clearing that was mostly empty except for a few tired cars. It felt abandoned, discarded, as if no one but Tanner and his roommates had squatted here for years. She'd never been inside his apartment—*the horror*, she couldn't imagine what it must smell like in there, he and his buddies and all their bright, sweaty Skechers stinking up the place—but she knew which one was his.

She parked and got out. Way out here, the night was cool and bright, but the vastness above her felt too close, like a roof about to collapse. In the distance, the hum and glow of the town lights sparkled beyond the trees, as though the battlefront of some obscure conflict lay just across the valley.

Hetta climbed the stairs, and from the landing she could see the red clay bank of the slope had been gouged away to accommodate the building. In the moonlight it looked necrotic, an abscess in the flesh of the hill. She went down the walkway to Tanner's apartment, Number Six, and paused at the big window. Someone moving inside caught her eye—in the kitchen, it seemed, they were going through cabinets. Somebody was up. That was good, though it wasn't Tanner; she could see this boy was full-sized, and his belly was way too big.

Hetta pounded on the door. "*Hello! Hey!*" Through the window, the dude in the kitchen didn't seem to notice. Tanner had told her how he and his roommates would stay up all night watching shitty movies, and get so drunk and stoned by the end they'd end up wrestling, and ruin half the furniture in the room just to feel something. Evidently the dude in the kitchen wasn't feeling much right now.

"*Hellooo*," she cooed, opening the door. "Just checking up on you boys." It was dark inside, but on the coffee table, there it was among the full ashtrays and the half-crushed beer cans—the VHS tape. It was the copy Tanner had made, she recognized his handwriting on the spine. She grabbed it, held it close.

In the kitchen, the young man didn't seem to understand he had a visitor. He was still going through the cabinets, looking for something. Hetta went around the partition, and stood in the kitchen doorway. "Pardon me, how we doin'?" She unconsciously adopted a slight mountain twang, maybe to make her presence here less alarming. "Is Tanner here?"

The big guy turned around—he was just a kid, like Tanner, but broader and thicker, a football player maybe, and she saw immediately his eyeballs were gone. Instead, there were two dark holes, the edges red and bothered as if he'd been digging at them with a utensil. Blood had dribbled down and covered most of the bottom half of his face. He held a coffee cup in his fist, but inside the cup, Hetta saw it wasn't coffee—it was the smushed, egg-white gobbets of his eyes. One of them bobbed, almost completely submerged, like a marshmallow in hot chocolate.

"*Uhh!*" Hetta grunted, and stepped back.

The big boy only moaned, and in the void of his mouth Hetta saw he had no tongue. Only a stub, a squirming slug sliced in two. And then he tipped the cup forward and took a sip of blood.

"*Fuck!*" Hetta backed into the living room. "What're you—"

She stopped, because she understood now they weren't alone. Her eyes had adjusted to the shadows: she turned and saw two figures in either corner, men bent over but facing inward toward the wall, like naughty students. Their broad backs were lumpy and twisted, and odd hats perched on their heads—tall and dirty and black, stovepipe hats similar to those Abraham Lincoln would wear. Their clothes were dark and ill-fitting. And a third man, Hetta saw now with a numb sense of panic, crouched in the far corner of the little dining area. Like the others, he huddled motionless with his nose facing in. The fists on his knees were as big as bricks. None of the men seemed to notice her at all—they were wholly focused on their own corners of the room.

The big boy in the kitchen still banged around, moaning through a mouthful of blood.

Hetta became aware of something else then—a wheeze, an airy hissing of some kind behind one of the closed doors. A bedroom. With an eye on the motionless men in the corners, she made herself take a step toward it. "*Tanner?*" she whispered. She put her hand on the doorknob and pushed.

A great gust ripped the door from her grasp then and slammed it open, and a gale hit her all at once—a raging, particulate wind, like a sandstorm. Reflexively she put a hand in front of her eyes and peeked through her fingers. A red, rusty glow washed over her, the color of daylight on Mars. When her eyes cleared, she beheld not a bedroom, but a staircase. Red-orange from the gloaming, rusted, rickety metal like a fire escape, the color of immense age. The frame of it was fastened by huge bolts to a rock wall, a sheer cliff-face to her left that seemed surreally, almost comically immense—it went up, beyond her sight, and down and down and down into dizzyingly fathomless depths. The rickety stairs themselves also went down and down—an impossible distance, miles from the look of things, with flat periodic landings descending all the way down, down, down into an immeasurable vastness that was eventually lost from sight in the strange orange mist or haze. It was like being above the clouds. The iron wind smelled of blood.

Hetta was darkly transfixed. She couldn't look away. As the haze roiled and reformed, through it she caught occasional glimpses of a vast landscape—a rim of bleak mountains, a cracked wasteland floor, impossible gorges and bridges spanning them, and in the dim distance, the jagged and aimless dirt-dauber spires of what looked like a city. The tangled geometry of steeples and minarets, the manner in which the mass of it appeared from her elevated vantage—it attacked her sense of proportion and symmetry, it was labyrinthine, hopelessly tangled, enormous blobs of buildings that seemed plopped onto smaller ones underneath like shat feces, factories belching black smoke from absurdly tilting stacks, arches and passages leading into far shadow. Boats crawled up fiery rivers under catwalks high above, and industrial ruins and viaducts glistened in the wet red mist. It was like an image in a picture book for demented children. To build this place, or even to inhabit it, you would surely have to be insane.

Something caught her eye, something moved far down the stairs, and Hetta watched as a tiny figure, dark-headed and slight, went down and down and down. The figure was taking the stairs two and three at a time. The back of his sports jersey was a huge bloodstain.

In the kitchen, the muscular kid let out a terrible moan, and from the edge of her gaze Hetta caught a sense of the three men in their corners slowly standing, turning, spinning around to regard her in the doorway. Something told her not to look at their faces. If she did, it might drive her mad. Her bladder shuddered, and she felt it go. She couldn't help herself— she fled, back out the front door and into the cool night of late spring, down the balcony and the stairs and across the parking lot.

***

She was almost to her car when the presence made itself known. Gravel crunched behind her, there was a hint of movement, a rustle of cloth, a hot wheeze of breath on her neck, and suddenly she knew she wasn't alone. She stopped. Running was no use. From the mass of it she knew it wasn't human. From the sound of the shuffling, the sheer displacement of the damp night air, it was something—some *thing*—very large. The nearness of it sizzled in her brain, a sense of dread zoomed up into microscopic levels, wrapping the world and bending the night around her with its gravity of fear, its density of despair. Despite a sudden shortness of breath, she took only shallow, heaving gasps—she didn't want to gulp in the foulness of everything around her. It took everything she had not to scream, or collapse into tears.

Goode evening, Hetta, a voice said, mostly in her mind. Gravelly and deep. Viscous and oozy. A strange accent she couldn't place, like Arabic mixed with…what? The redneck south? She didn't turn around. She wiped her mouth. Her spit tasted like copper.

"What?" she coughed out. It was all she could manage.

By my deeds thou knowest me, Hetta. I am He who joined the rebellion, He who commands thirtie legions, paladin & blackguarde. I am He who sparred with the greate Dark Knight, who gave of himselfe to Oto Benga for over a centurie, I am He who did strewe the shattered souls of young warriors like ashes over the compasse of the four parts of the globe of Heaven, Ayre, Earth, & Hell, I am He who advised & misadvised the myriad princes and kinges, I am He who started wars of Heaven & Earth, Encroacher, Usurper, the Wielder of Stormes, the Deposer of all thinges humaine & the crusher of fieldes of wheat. Why have ye called to me?

The instinct to turn around blazed inside of her, her thoughts boiling and scalding and only half-recognizable, but she knew she couldn't. Not unless she wanted to end up like Tanner's roommate in there, with her eyes plucked from her skull like grapes from a bowl. Or worse.

"Wh—where's my friend?" she stammered, even though she already knew the answer. "Where's Tanner?" She could hear the creature's breathing, if that's what you called it. In her mind's eye an image flashed—a vision of herself in the gravel parking lot, the glow of the small town in the distance, and behind her a great humanoid with the head of a bird, atop a great black wolf. She almost passed out from the thought of it alone.

"What do you want?" she asked. The gravity that held her to the ground seemed to loosen, the mass of it opened from above, and she went up on tiptoe and struggled not to go airborne, the fear rising inside her with the blood-mist in the air. She could hardly breathe now.

It was thou who willed me, the demon said, not unkindly. *Thou, in whose sight all thinges vissible & invissible are open & manifest to me, in whose presence are all thinges foull & spoiled, & from whome noe seecret is hid, unto whome everie hart is open & to whome everie soule doth confesse it selff, & everie tong doth damn & afflict thy shame upon whome all thinges doubtfull, even those unknowen & whoose neede to hide is manifest & open, of whose unspeakable terror the Heavens & the Earth & Infernall doth observe. Obayinge my will & commaundements with all dilligence, faithfully & truly to their uttermost powers without the hurt of my body, soule, mind, or goods or anie livinge creatures whatsoever, or whersoever, & further with thy help, I require thee to geve me leave & lysence to have to my kin, the companie of thy holy & blessed Aungells, which I doe or shall everherafter binde & loosse bringinge to my obedience all those spirits which were throwen out of heaven for their pride & disobedience, that they accomplish my will & commaundements faithfully truly & justly to their uttermoste powers presently & speedily. I do not come for everione, nor even when the summonning is worthie. But you, Hetta Salter, in thy worcks, thou art worthie.*

I am worthie, Hetta thought stupidly. In her befuddlement it made her feel good despite the rancid, spoiled quality of the world around her. Then her brain snagged on something. *Nor even when the summonning is worthie?*

"Wait—our summoning was unworthy?" She was now fully aloft. The toes of her shoes drifted in the air. Her brain didn't want to work, but she forced it. "Are you saying...we—we didn't get the ceremony right?"

There was no answer. Down the hill, the road was quiet. The night had a frozen quality, as if the moments of it had ground to a halt. It felt as if this stillness was the true way of things, rather than the endless tumble of moment upon moment, but then a slight breeze blew in a touch of chill from the mountains. It didn't refresh the air. Suspended a few inches above the ground now, she could feel the putrid bulk of the presence behind her, even though the flat wash of the parking lot floodlights revealed no shadow other than her own. "How am I worthy?"

Thy heart is blacke, Hetta Salter, & thy aimes ambitious. Thou wouldst thrive in the fyery fornaces of my realm.

Hetta didn't know if that was a compliment or not. "What are you going to do?"

She could almost hear him smile, if a demon with a beak could smile. The words rang in her head: *I will fulfill thy wish.*

"Even though we got the ceremony wrong," she confirmed, "you'll do as I want?" There was no response. Despite her fear, she felt the need to press the point. "You'll do it?"

If this man views your worke, he will die. By his own hand.

"And be taken to Hell."

But thou must saye it.

She closed her eyes. Through the whirling vortex of her fear, the smell came to her—viscera and squirming offal and putrid flesh. And mud—deep, wet, stinking, defiled mud. Bacterial mud. Plague mud.

"I wish it," she said.

There was nothing else. And she knew it: now she was alone. Her heels touched solid ground again. The night was cool, almost wintry. And fresh, the air was weirdly fresh. The stars above burned clear and cold. She felt something in her hand, and realized she still held the VHS tape.

Down on the road, a lone car approached, and then slid past like a last breath.

***

On her way home, she could feel the difference already. As though the world had changed in a heartbeat, slipped its tracks, or maybe had been like that the whole time and she never knew. The paper mill, which was the tiny town's biggest employer other than the college itself, stood stark in the shadows of the night, its smokestacks belching white breath, just like those in the far-off cities of the vision she'd seen in Tanner's apartment. As she drove, Hetta felt someone watching her, way up high, on one of the catwalks. She turned to see a lone silhouette, stark against the smoke, raise a hand as she passed.

Halfway to the city, as she crept along on the four-lane that wound through the hills, a man beside the road caught her eye. He was masturbating in the middle of a fenced-in basketball court. It was well past two AM, but he waved jovially to her as her car went by. "*Hettaaaaahh!*" he yelled, "*thaaaannnk you!*" and then she was past.

Closer in to the city, on a side street not far from her apartment, a gang of hoodlums were harassing or celebrating some poor homeless man, it was hard to tell. But one of the boys turned to her and waved. He had only one arm. In the streetlights, it looked to her like the rims of his eyes were empty, but somehow he knew her all the same.

When she got home, she plodded up the stairs and went inside her apartment. Just then the hallway door downstairs, which stayed locked due to the economic uncertainties of the neighborhood, rattled hard with several insistent knocks: *BOOM BOOM BOOM*. Nervously, her breath catching in her throat, Hetta opened her front door and made herself peek around the corner and down the stairs. The door was closed and locked. The one window was dark and empty.

Wasted, she went back inside, fell into bed, and slept like a corpse.

***

When she woke up, she got herself a glass of water in the kitchen, and downed it in a gulp. Tanner was gone. Not a single word from him, nor from anyone who knew him. His texts were missing on her phone. Not just gone—negated, as if Tanner had never been there at all.

The VHS box sat on the counter in her kitchen, warping the gravity of the world. She could tell it was evil. It looked like any other tape—the dated graphics on the cover like a hangover from the 80's. The insipidity of it disguised its true intentions. But when she picked it up, it felt heavier, weightier, sturdier, as though there were more in the box than just an old tape. It felt solid, like a brick.

She put it in the front room and wrestled open the window, and avoided that area for the rest of the day. Let it foul up the neighborhood, she thought, let it stink up the world. Later that night, she leaned against the wall and watched it, making sure it didn't try to worm its way back into her bedroom. Or, god forbid, back into her own collection of old VHS tapes. That would be hilarious.

***

Two days later, she took the tape to Hensley's office, carrying it with two fingers away from herself, down empty hallways and up dreary stairwells and through lonely common rooms. Finals were next week, school was almost out now, everything was on skeleton crew. She knocked on Hensley's door, feeling like the tape was shouting to her, screaming at her, it was blistering her, exhilarating and terrible. But Hensley never answered.

She took it to the department secretary, a middle-aged woman named Joyce who'd never really liked Hetta. That was okay, when Hetta was head of the department, Joyce would be packing her bags. "Can I leave this with you?" Hetta said sweetly, holding up the tape. It seemed to whisper to her, to try to seduce her. *Watch me*, it seemed to murmur, *consume me*. Or maybe that was only in her head. Hetta kept her face slack, to not show any strain at all. "For Dr. Hensley. And *only* Dr. Hensley."

Joyce shrugged. "Sure."

Hetta grabbed a sticky note from Joyce's desk, and wrote, HETTA J. SALTER SHORT FILM. 8:59:29 FOR DR. HENSLEY *ONLY*.

She underlined *only* a few times. Joyce put the tape aside and went back to her work. The tape sat on the desk, looking innocuous, harmless, bland as a boat shoe. But inside it were the *fyery fornaces* of Hell.

The next time she saw Hensley, he would be in a coffin.

Hetta was halfway home when she made the U-turn. *Fuck fuck fuck*, she thought. She sped back to campus, rushed up the stairs as if on a wind, and into Joyce's office. The tape was still there on the desk, a few envelopes and letters sitting atop it now, steeping in the tape's aura of malice. There was no one here, anyone could have picked it up, anyone could have been sent straight to Hell. It was too dangerous. Hetta snatched it, and was gone.

***

It took her three days to get the tape directly into Hensley's hands. He'd been at some conference or other, but now he was back and strolling the halls, carrying books and hitching his corduroys with one hand and hurrying from one place to the next. Hetta managed to stop him for thirty seconds or so, and sheepishly handed the tape over. He took it without looking at it. "Yes, yes, how exciting, a horror film, wow, thanks so much!" he said, and then he was gone down the hall and around the corner.

The following morning, the phone woke her up. Since the ceremony, her sleep had been wonderful, velvety, the vast, voided sleep of nothingness. But she was due a telephone call just about exactly right now.

It was Hensley's secretary, Joyce. "Hetta," Joyce said in a thin, quavery voice. Joyce's nasal bleat was always thin, with a prim southern pep that grated against nearly everyone. But this morning it sounded thinner and less peppy than ever before. "Are you there?"

"I'm here," Hetta croaked, trying to sound more awake than she really was. It was early. She pushed herself up on one elbow. "Yeah, what's up?"

"Uh…" Joyce started, and then stopped. "I'm calling all the faculty and the teachers." Her voice hitched, and then she said, "Walt's dead, Hetta. It was a fire. And he's dead."

"A what?" Hetta sat up further, trying to think. She tried to convey her surprise, but it sounded more like grim fascination.

"His daughter. She burned herself up, they think it was her. And she burned up the whole family. Walt's wife is dead, too. And their five-year-old daughter. Little Tess. Oh God."

"*What?*" Hetta's tongue was thick. She wiped her mouth on the collar of her t-shirt, leaving a spit-stain. Joyce's words seemed to hang visible in the air. "That's…that's horrible."

On the other end of the phone, a little mewling sound told her that Joyce had started to cry.

By nine AM, the news came on, and there it was. The daughter had indeed burned herself up, and the whole family with her. The jerky little news video on Hetta's laptop blared the latest: "College town reels from house fire. Multiple fatalities. Arson suspected." And there was footage—a nice neighborhood, golf course lawns, noble trees. And the ruined, smoking husk of a grand house. It had once been two stories, constructed in the Tudor style, but now the upper story was simply…gone. It looked as though a bomb had exploded Firemen came and went in the clear morning.

Hetta reeled into the kitchen and got an ice cube out of the freezer, and put it against her neck. The whole family? Jeez, that wasn't part of the plan. That little girl, his little blonde daughter, in Hell? Her heart thudded, she felt a little sick.

By noon, the news had developed. There were multiple fires now in the county. *Officials are working hard to contain a series of arson fires last night and this morning near UNSC,* the article said. *At least nine homes have suffered catastrophic damage, and multiple fatalities are being reported in what local officials are calling a coordinated attack. The motive behind the series of fires has not been determined, but evidence is being collected, and as of now is being treated as possible domestic terrorism. Autopsies will be conducted to determine the identity of the victims and cause of death. We expect to have additional information to release once the fire-scene searches are completed.*

Multiple fatalities? Were these connected to her? A feeling of dread circled round and round with the annoyance of an angry wasp. Hetta got back in bed and closed her eyes and pulled her covers up. A migraine beat at the doors of her brain, trying to get in.

***

By one PM she had a passable, plausible theory. Somehow Hensley's daughter had seen the video. By what manner, she didn't know. And the multiple fires, she couldn't figure them out, either. Was Hensley having a house party or something, with everyone watching her tape? That seemed unlikely, yet there it was.

But by two PM, more fires were reported, including in the city, not far from her apartment. More fatalities, more arson. Hetta went outside and stood on the hot sidewalk and watched the smoke rising into the sky from a few blocks over. Sirens called out, just over there, and from the sound of things, other areas, too. Mystified, Hetta went back upstairs and searched on her computer. Fires were sprouting all over the city, spreading like dandelions on a spring morning.

What the hell? Surely that had nothing to do with her. The Andras curse was confined to that one tape. Right? *Right?*

Unless someone had digitized it.

Surely Tanner hadn't fucked up that bad, had he?

It shouldn't matter. The Andras demon-seed wouldn't bloom without the 29.97 frames. The effect was confined to that one VHS tape. If it had ever been digitized, if anyone was stupid enough to do that, it would lose any power it possessed.

Probably. Probably it would lose any power it possessed.

Fuck fuck fuck, Hetta thought. She did a frantic search for Hensley's daughter on the internet. She tried to get her thoughts together. Hensley had shown her a picture before, and mentioned the girl's name. Candy, Mandy, Brandy, something like that. Hetta went into the kitchen, and with shaking hands made herself a cup of coffee. Then she had it: *Sandy*, the girl's name was Sandy. She hurried back to her laptop, and did a search for *Sandy Hensley J. Walter Hensley.*

Nothing.

Well, almost nothing. Way down the page was a link for a YouTube account. When Hetta clicked it, she saw with a feeling like an earthquake in her gut that her own film, *What We Talk About When We Talk About Hemoglobin*, was there. It was right there. The video had been uploaded at 8:59 last night. *WaTcH tHiS!* Sandy Hensley had written. *ToO fUnNy!*

SoOoO bAd!!!

With a feeling of growing doom, Hetta looked at the girl's followers: 31,000. Evidently Sandy had been something of a child prodigy in piano, just like her dad. This had brought her a modest measure of local fame. When she'd uploaded it, it had apparently posted simultaneously to Facebook, YouTube, Instagram, and Twitter.

Sandy's friends. Her friends were watching it. And her 31,000 fans.

Hetta put her face down on the scratched wood of her kitchen table and closed her eyes. A vein pounded in her temple. The migraine had settled itself around her brain like a boa constrictor.

***

In less than an hour, the thing had gone viral.

Sick! the kids were saying. *So terrible! Worse than* The Room.*!!*

The Room. Hetta had heard of that film, but had never seen it. Evidently it was an object of worldwide scorn. She sat in the front room with the blinds down and picked at the arm of the chair until her nail bled. She and Tanner had gotten the ceremony wrong. Andras himself had said so, but he'd agreed to do it anyway. Hetta was certain he would have been bound by the same terms of the ceremony. He would have been bound by the 29.97 frames. But maybe not?

By three PM she had her answer. The video had over 9,000 views on YouTube alone. By three-thirty, it was 21,000.

That's when the fires started in earnest.

By four PM, Nashville was on fire. By four-thirty, it was Dallas. By five PM, it was Santa Fe and Albuquerque. By six PM, it was LA. Hetta watched on her laptop as the breaking news chyrons scrolled past. *Cities on Flame*, it said. *Thousands feared dead.*

… and sent to Hell, she finished. She turned off the TV, and picked up her phone. She opened the YouTube app, and searched for *Hemoglobin short film*. It came up immediately, in multiple links. It had spread even more. She saw the views clicking higher every second. 73K now.

The comments were hilarious, if you liked that kind of thing. *Funniest piece of shit in forever!* JamieWhoa69 said. *So stewpid you gotta watch it!* joeydabarbarian said. *The new* Birdemic, Muddymambo enthused. *You'll be in tears in less than a minute! Watch all the way to the end!*

Hetta rubbed her eyes. The migraine was in full hailstorm now at the back of her skull. She felt feverish. This was not how it was supposed to go. Not at all.

When she checked it again, the views were up to 111K. And when she counted, she found fourteen separate links—her video, her noisy shitty low-res VHS movie, fourteen unique copies of her short film. People were watching it all over the web.

It was kids, mostly. Who else had time to watch YouTube? Kids, burning themselves up, immolating themselves, and often their families. Their souls sent straight to Hell and damnation eternal. She imagined that rickety staircase going down, down, down, full of teenagers marching to that insane city below.

"Andras," Hetta said out loud. It sounded oddly normal in the room. "You fucker."

A miserable stillness lay over everything. Sirens called out from far away. Her headache boomed. Worst of all, from what she'd gathered, Hensley had never even seen it. Hetta sat back in her lumpy chair and stared at the title frame of her film. *What We Talk About When We Talk About Hemoglobin,* it said. Outside, someone sobbed, wailing like a lonely coyote.

Fuck fuck fuck, Hetta thought, and leaned forward to her laptop, and hit play.

about the author

Polly Schattel is a writer and filmmaker living in Asheville, NC.

Lightning Source UK Ltd.
Milton Keynes UK
UKHW042202150223
417096UK00010B/135